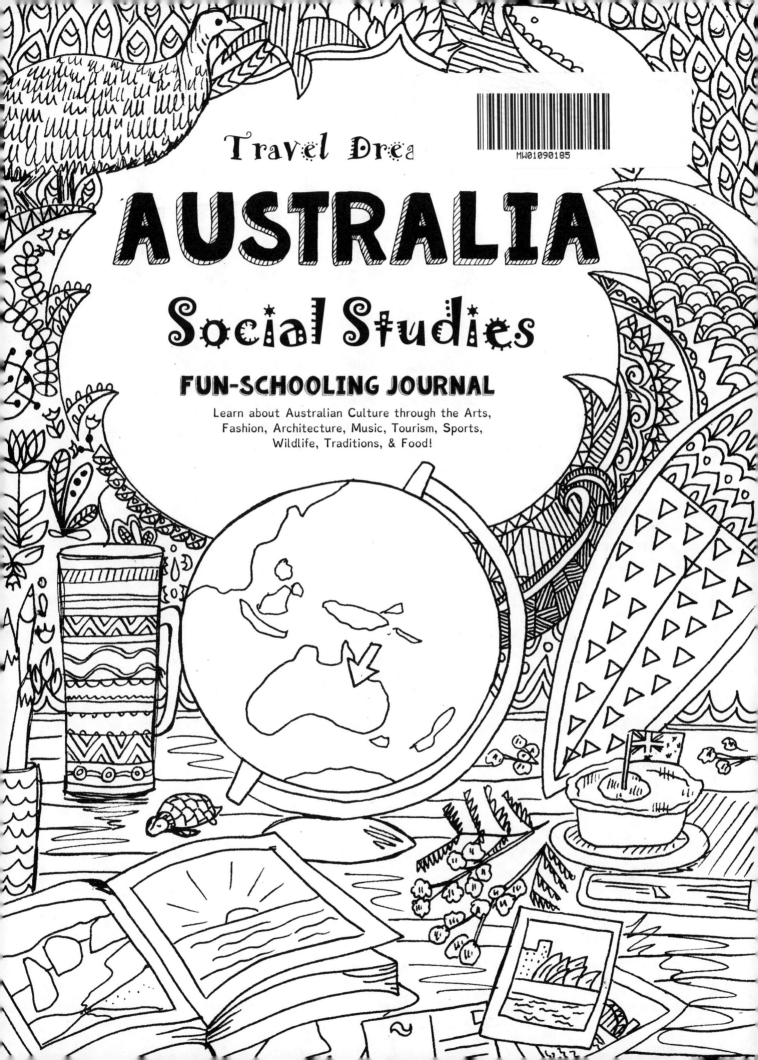

Travel Drea

AUSTRALIA

Social Studies

FUN-SCHOOLING JOURNAL

Learn about Australian Culture through the Arts,
Fashion, Architecture, Music, Tourism, Sports,
Wildlife, Traditions, & Food!

To hear traditional music from this country listen to

Travel Dreams Geography

AROUND THE WORLD
IN 14 SONGS

Search for Amazon Product Number: B072C2QXJS

Around the world in **14** songs is a delightful musical tour of the world. Adults and children will enjoy these original instrumental songs that reflect the authentic style of music that originated on all six major continents. Travel to the rhythm and melody of traditional instruments, and enjoy the fun-filled tunes.

The musical journey begins in Ireland, sweeps across Europe, dances through Asia, Africa and then soars over the ocean to Australia and the Caribbean! After an exciting night at a Smoky Mountain bluegrass festival you will enjoy a siesta in Mexico and finally land in Brazil where you will join the festa in Rio-De-Janeiro.

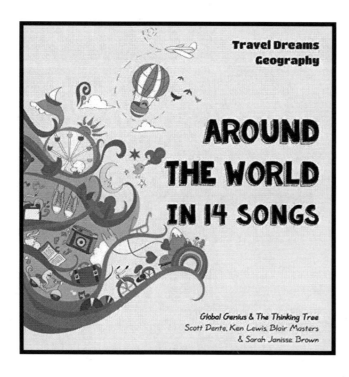

Music has never been more fun... or educational!

Travel Dreams

AUSTRALIA

FUN-SCHOOLING
JOURNAL

An Adventurous Approach
Social Studies

Learn about Australian Culture Through the Arts,
Fashion, Architecture, Music, Tourism, Sports,
Wildlife, Traditions, & Food!

Travel Dreams
AUSTRALIA
FUN-SCHOOLING
Journal

Name:

Date:

Contact Information:

About Me:

Let's Learn!

Topics & Activities You Can Explore With This Curriculum:

- Ethnic Cooking
- Travel
- History of Interesting Places
- How People Live
- Tourism
- Transportation
- Wildlife and Natural Wonders
- Cultural Traditions
- Natural Disasters

- Famous and Interesting People
- Missionary Stories
- Scientific Discoveries
- Fashion
- Architecture
- Plants
- Animals
- Maps
- Language

AUSTRALIA

AUSTRALIA

Travel Dreams Fun-School Journal

You are going to learn about Australia

Teacher & Parent To-Do List:

- Plan a trip to Australia or just plan a trip to the library or local bookstore.
- Download Google Earth so your child can zoom in and learn more!
- Choose online videos about Australia so your child can learn about culture, food, tourism, traditions, and history.
- Be prepared to help your child choose an ethnic recipe and shop for the ingredients.

Go to the Library or Bookstore to Pick Out:

- Books about Australia
- One Atlas or Book of Maps
- One Colorful Cookbook with Recipes from Australia

DRAW THE COVER OF YOUR BOOKS!

COLOR IN AUSTRALIA ON THE MAP

Zoom into Australia using Google Earth and explore
the wonders of this amazing country!

LABEL THE MAP
Add 15 Interesting Things to this Map!

Write or Draw

Use your Library Books

Popular Foods:	Traditional Clothing:

Draw the Flag:	A Quote or Proverb:

A Historic Event:	A Famous Landmark:

LEARNING TIME

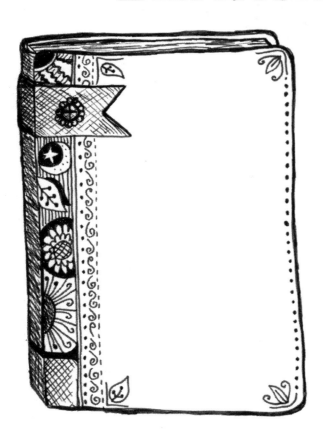

READ A BOOK AND WATCH A VIDEO ABOUT FOOD IN AUSTRALIA:

BOOK TITLE:_____
_____
VIDEO TITLE: _____
_____
_____

What did you Learn?
_____
_____
_____
_____
_____
_____

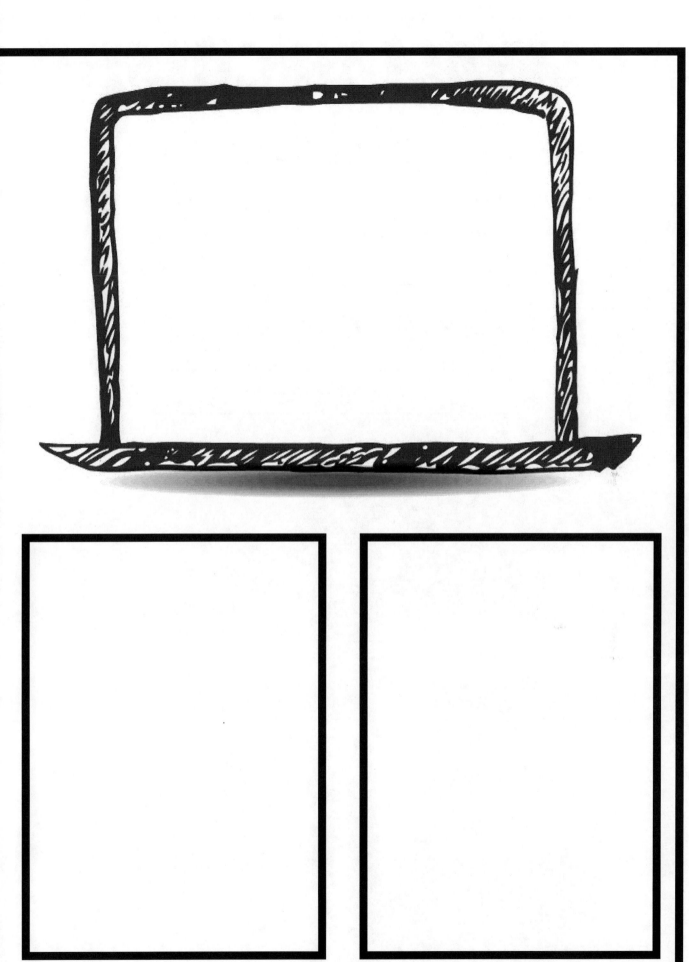

AUSTRALIAN CUISINE

What do Australians love to eat?

Can you list **5** of the most popular Australian dishes?

1. _____
2. _____
3. _____
4. _____
5. _____

Draw your favorite Australian food

Find a Recipe From
AUSTRALIA

TITLE:

_____

Ingredients:

_____   _____

_____   _____

_____   _____

_____   _____

_____   _____

Instructions:

_____

_____

_____

_____

_____

_____

_____

_____

_____

Step by Step Food Prep:

1	2
3	4
5	6

**DRAW
THE FOOD
THAT YOU
PREPARED!**

**RATE THE
RESULTS!
1, 2, 3, 4, 5**

Color the words
that best describe
your food:

DELICIOUS
YUMMY
TASTY
GREAT
DELIGHTFUL
OKAY
BLAH!
GROSS
YUCKY
DISGUSTING
STINKY
ICKY

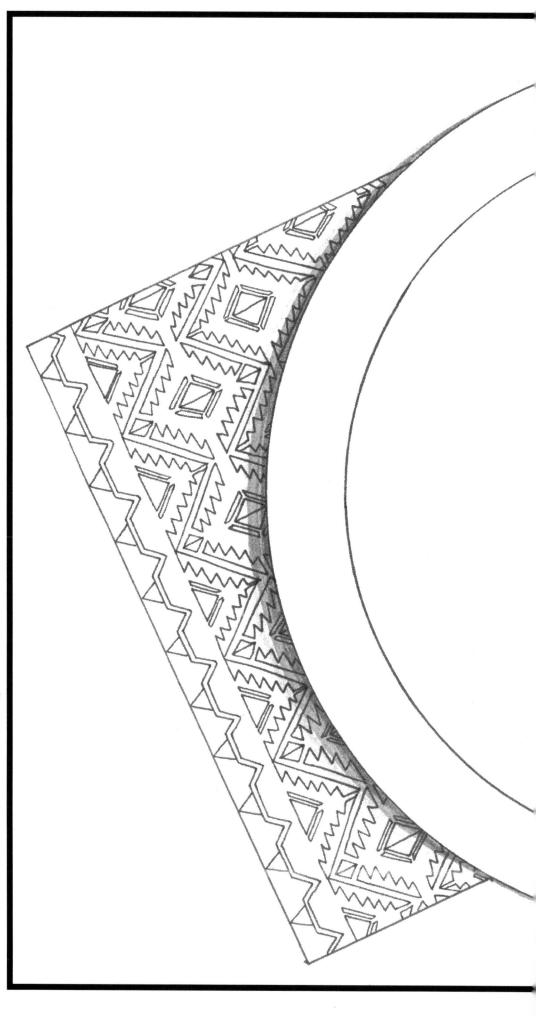

What to Do in Australia

Create a **COMIC STRIP** showing your dream adventure!

LEARNING TIME

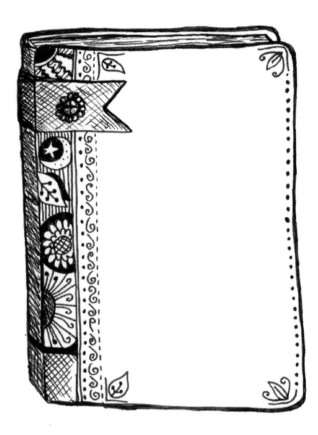

READ A BOOK AND WATCH A VIDEO ABOUT A FAMOUS PERSON

BOOK TITLE:_____
_____
VIDEO TITLE: _____
_____
_____

Write 3 Interesting Biography Facts
_____
_____
_____
_____
_____
_____

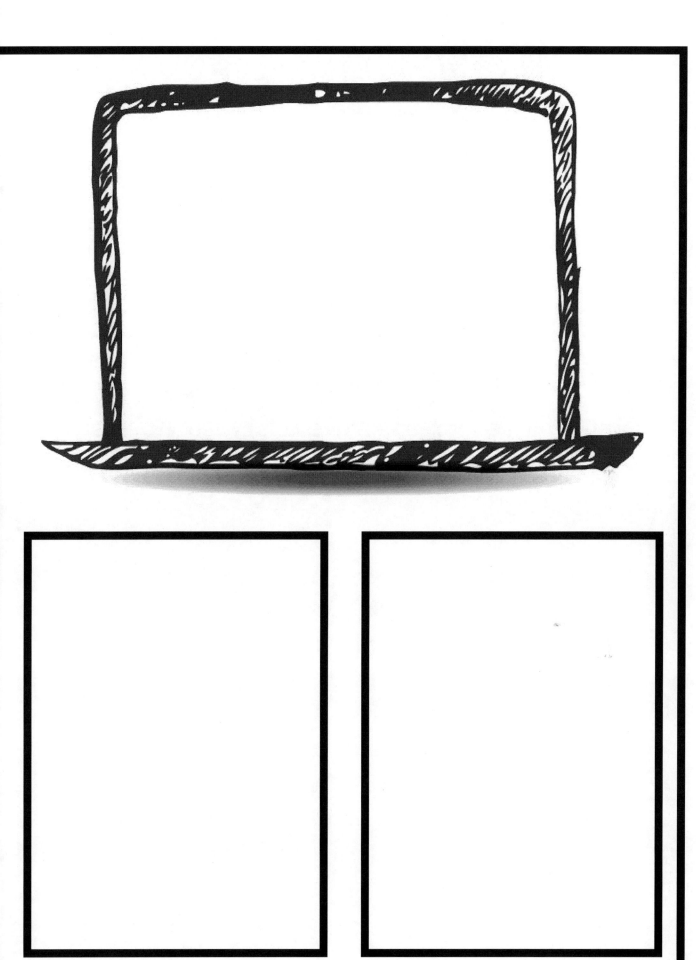

All About Style

AUSTRALIA

Fashion in the City

_____

_____

_____

MODERN STYLES

Draw yourself dressed like a stylish Australian:

Color The Traditional Costume:

Trace and color this
traditional Female Australian costume

Trace and color this traditional male Australian costume

AUSTRALIAN HISTORY

Write about a Historic Event

_____

_____

_____

_____

_____

_____

_____

_____

_____

_____

_____

_____

_____

_____

LEARNING TIME

READ A BOOK AND WATCH A VIDEO ABOUT NATURE & WILDLIFE

BOOK TITLE:_____
_____
VIDEO TITLE: _____
_____
_____

Notes:
_____
_____
_____
_____
_____
_____

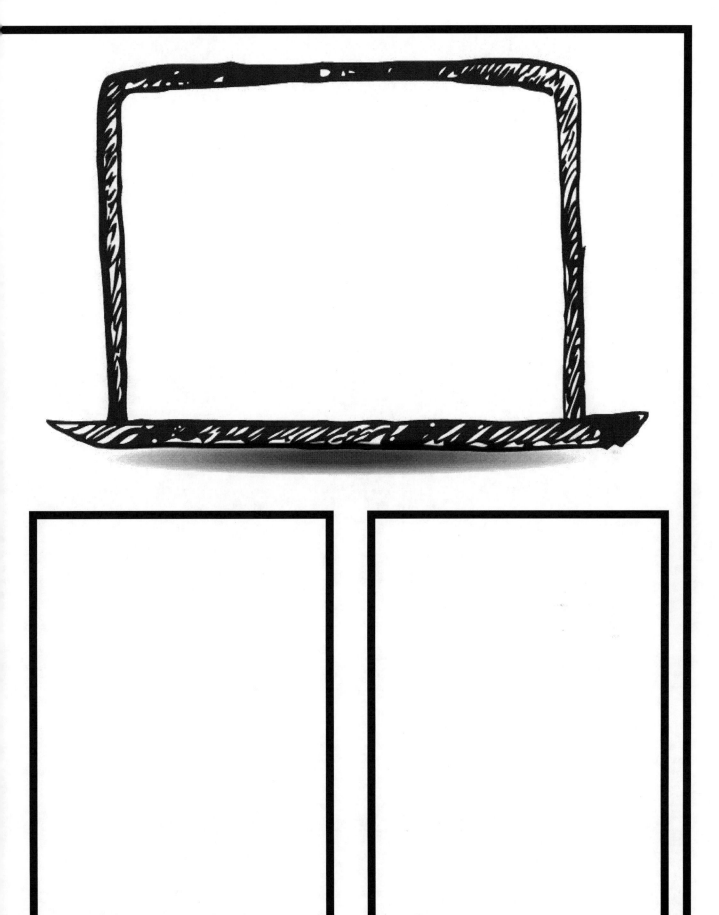

WHat ANiMaLS LiVe iN AUStRaLia?
CaN yoU LiSt teN?

1. _____

2. _____

3. _____

4. _____

5. _____

6. _____

7. _____

8. _____

9. _____

10. _____

Draw each of the animals

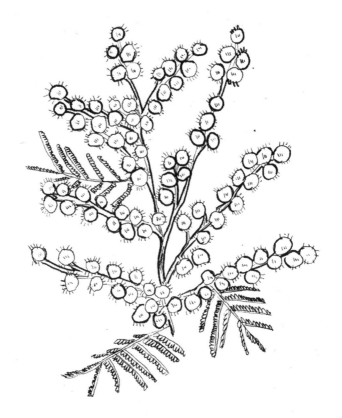

PLANTS IN AUSTRALIA

Can you list ten flowers or trees found in Australia?

1._____

2._____

3._____

4._____

5._____

6._____

7._____

8._____

9._____

10._____

Draw each of the plants

HISTORY OF MUSIC IN AUSTRALIA

Write about a famous Australian musician:

_____

_____
_____
_____
_____
_____
_____
_____

What instrument did he/she play?

_____

Can you draw it?

A NATIONAL INSTRUMENT

To hear traditional music from this country listen to
Travel Dreams Geography—Around the World in **14** Songs

Track Number & Song Name:
10-Australia – The Bungle Bungle

AUSTRALIAN ART & ENTERTAINMENT

Read a book or Watch a documentary about art and entertainment in Australia

Write down 5 interesting things you learned :

1. _____
_____

2. _____
_____

3. _____
_____

4. _____
_____

5. _____
_____

Draw or doodle in Australian Style

Write doWN a quote or a Lyric From a FaMous AustraLian poeM or Song

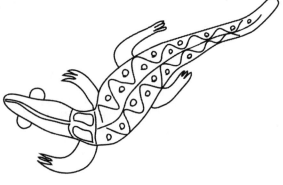

_____

_____

_____

_____

_____

_____

_____

_____

_____

_____

_____

_____

HISTORY OF TRANSPORTATION IN AUSTRALIA

Find 3 interesting Facts about Australian transportation

1. _____

_____

_____

2. _____

_____

_____

3. _____

_____

_____

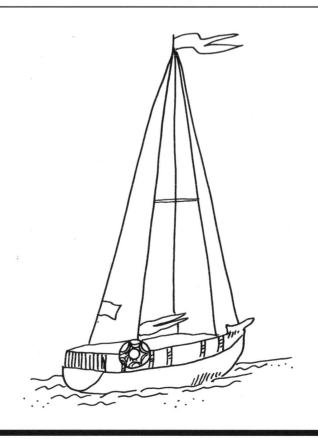

Use your imagination and add something to this picture.

Write a short story about this picture

_____

_____

_____

_____

_____

_____

_____

_____

AUSTRALIAN INVENTIONS

Read a book or Watch a documentary about your Favorite Australian inventor:

_____

Write down 5 interesting things about his/her life:

1. _____

2. _____

3. _____

4. _____

5. _____

Write down 3 Australian inventions that changed the world:

1. _____

2. _____

3. _____

Draw your Favorite Australian invention

AN AUSTRALIAN ATHLETE

Read a book or Watch a documentary about your Favorite Australian Athlete:

_____

Write down 5 interesting things about his/her life:

1._____
_____

2._____
_____

3._____
_____

4._____
_____

5._____
_____

DraW A Sport that is popular in Australia

AUSTRALIAN HOMES

Write about a family tradition in Australia

_____

_____

_____

_____

AUSTRALIAN TRADITIONS

Draw some traditional Australian décor elements

Trace & Color
A TRADITIONAL AUSTRALIAN HOME

Design Your Own
AUSTRALIAN HOME

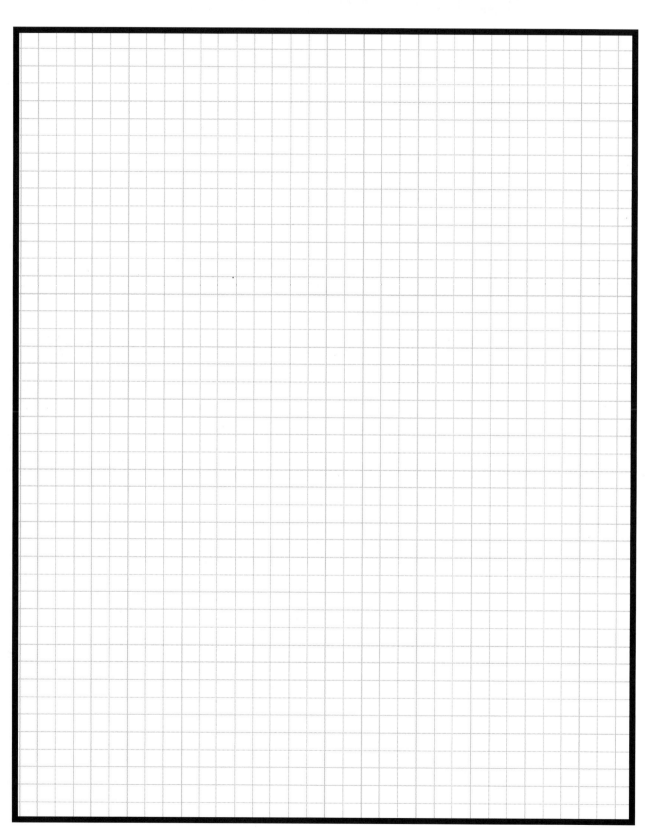

FiND aND COLOr iN THE HiDDEN ObjECTS

LEARNING TIME

READ A BOOK AND WATCH A VIDEO ABOUT TOURISM & TRAVEL

BOOK TITLE:_____
_____
VIDEO TITLE: _____
_____
_____

Notes:
_____
_____
_____
_____
_____
_____

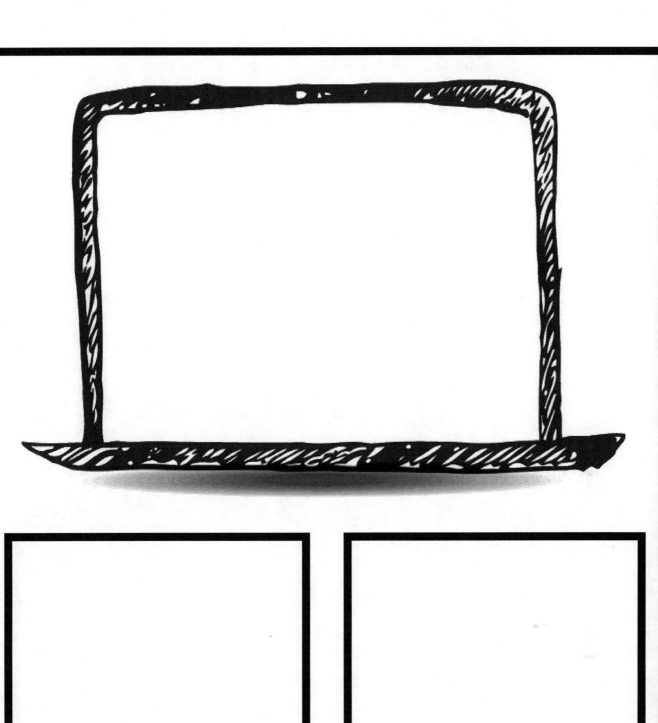

PLAN A TRIP TO THE CAPITAL OF AUSTRALIA

━ ━ ━ ━ ━ ━

Who are you going with?

_____

What are you taking with you?

_____

How long is your trip?

_____

What do you want to see or visit?

_____

What to Do in Sydney

Five Things to Know when Traveling to
AUSTRALIA

1 _____

2 _____

3 _____

4 _____

5 _____

What to Say

Create a **COMIC STRIP** using six unique Australian phrases:

CREATIVE WRITING

Write a story about an imaginary trip to Australia

Illustrate your Story

Do it Yourself
HOMESCHOOL
JOURNALS
BY THE THINKING TREE, LLC

Made in United States
Orlando, FL
10 January 2025

56754839R10037